Great Careers for People Interested in
The Past

by
Victoria Vincent

An imprint of Gale Research,
An ITP Information/Reference Group Company

Changing the Way the World Learns

NEW YORK • LONDON • BONN • BOSTON • DETROIT • MADRID
MELBOURNE • MEXICO CITY • PARIS • SINGAPORE • TOKYO
TORONTO • WASHINGTON • ALBANY NY • BELMONT CA • CINCINNATI OH

© 1996
Trifolium Books Inc. and Weigl Educational Publishers Limited

First published in Canada by Trifolium Books Inc. and Weigl
Educational Publishers Limited

U•X•L is the exclusive publisher of the U.S. library edition of Series 3.

U·X·L

An imprint of
Gale Research
835 Penobscot Bldg.
Detroit, MI 48226

Library of Congress Catalog Card Number 95-62266
ISBN 0-7876-0861-0

Acknowledgments
The author and the publishers wish to thank those
people whose careers are featured in this book for
allowing us to interview and photograph them at
work. Their love for their chosen careers has
made our task an enjoyable one.

The author would especially like to thank Jon
Jouppien for his assistance in tracking down
sources. Sincere thanks also goes to Cam Tsujita
and Simeon Marcano for their cooperation. The
author would also like to thank the Royal Ontario
Museum, Jon Jouppien, Jennifer Dunn, Charlotte
Dean, and Jim Retallack for allowing us to use
photos from their collections. Special thanks to
Ted Krieg, owner of Comic Connection, for
letting us disrupt business on two busy Saturdays
to take pictures.

Design concept: Julian Cleva
Design and layout: Warren Clark, Karen Dudley
Editors: Ann Downar, Rosemary Tanner
Project coordinator, proofreader: Diane Klim
Production coordinator: Amanda Woodrow
Content review: Mary Kay Winter, Julie Czerneda

Printed and bound in Canada
10 9 8 7 6 5 4 3 2 1

This book's text stock contains more than 50% recycled paper.

Contents

Featured profiles

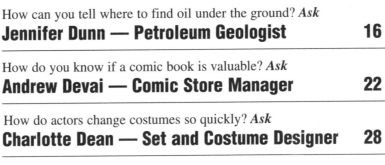

Careers at a glance

Melanie Fernandez

Museum Coordinator

PERSONAL PROFILE

Career: Coordinator of a "hands-on" gallery, a small museum within a larger museum.

Interests: Art, cooking, travel. "I particularly like learning about contemporary North American First Nations art."

Latest accomplishment: "I recently received a Smithsonian fellowship. This will enable me to assist in the development of a permanent exhibition on 19th-century history. The exhibition will deal with the different perspectives about the history of that time."

Why I do what I do: "I've always loved the museum. I've always been drawn to the past."

I am: Curious and friendly. "I like to work with people and I have a lot of energy."

What I wanted to be when I was in school: "A veterinarian. I've always had lots of pets."

What a museum coordinator does

"**I** coordinate!" says Melanie Fernandez. "My job covers everything to do with one gallery in a major museum." She dreams up new ideas and organizes the people who work in the gallery. She also makes sure that she knows what programs are going on in the rest of the museum so her gallery can participate.

"This is a hands-on gallery where visitors can handle objects from the past and learn about them," explains Melanie. "The gallery opened 11 years ago. We started because the scientists and curators wanted to share the information about the collections in a more interactive way.

Working with the past

One thing that Melanie coordinates is how the objects from the past are displayed in the gallery. "We spend a lot of time dreaming up new displays for our visitors to use. We want the gallery to make them curious about the past. That way, they will start to look for answers on why the past was the way it was. Most visitors don't realize how much work and thought we put into this process."

A part of a larger whole

An important part of Melanie's job is keeping up with what happens in the rest of the museum, and in the world in general. This means many committee meetings to discuss issues that affect the museum and its collections.

For example, respecting the environment has become an important topic in recent years. "Right now, there is a lot of concern about our exhibitions of plants and animals from all over the world. In the past, no one minded when samples of butterflies or birds or insects were collected for museums. Now, people realize that we can't just go and take what we want. We have to protect the environment and make sure these species survive in the wild. The museum also carefully looks after and studies the natural history collections that we already have. We can't replace them!"

"We have to protect the objects in the collection," says Melanie. "We don't use any reproductions in our exhibits."

Planning displays

Melanie is constantly thinking of new ways to display the museum's collections so that they won't be damaged when the visitors handle them. In her gallery, the displays are touchable, something you usually don't find in a museum. Each display begins with a plan like the one shown here. Then many people — artists, conservators, builders — contribute their expertise to make the finished display.

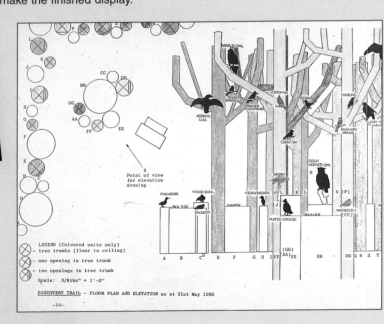

All in a day's work

"No two days are ever the same here. My workday depends on what is happening in the gallery and in the rest of the museum." Although the museum staff has regular hours, Melanie's working hours can vary quite a bit. That means working evenings and weekends. "Sometimes I come in to work on weekends just because it is quiet. During the week, every morning and every afternoon, we have a classroom full of kids in the gallery, using the displays. Some of the staff are always involved in explaining things."

Taking care of the collections

When they are not talking to young visitors, Melanie and her staff spend time caring for the objects in the gallery. "Our display material comes from other areas of the museum. We ask the other departments to loan it to us. At first, they weren't sure if they wanted to do this, but we have a really good track record of taking care of the collections."

Even with care, things do get broken. Melanie has learned a lot about gluing bits and pieces of animals back together. "There is always something that needs to be fixed. I'm very good at gluing the legs back on bugs." She says this skill is also useful at home. "I can fix anything I drop on the floor!"

A lot depends on the weather

The museum's first priority is its visitors. Bad weather brings both the slowest and busiest days around the museum. "It's boring when a snowstorm hits and no one can come in. We close about one day a year because of weather."

Still, bad weather of another kind brings in a flood of visitors. "During the summer, if it rains, we know it's going to be busy. There's less to do outside so many people come here." On those days, the staff is kept busy just seeing to the visitors, and it is difficult to get anything else done.

A display case showing antique lace from different parts of the world. This display encourages students to look up the answers to their questions in a nearby reference file.

Mayan weaving. Made by a Guatemalan woman, the pattern in this fabric tells a story. Each symbol has a meaning. The traditional patterns are passed down from generation to generation.

Teaching

Melanie spends part of each day teaching what she knows to others. Staff from other museums visit regularly to learn how the gallery presents its material. Melanie gives lectures in Museum Studies, teaching how to prepare displays and care for the collections.

She also supervises co-op students who want to make museum work their career. "We usually have about 20 co-op students each year in the museum — only one in the gallery. They earn high school credits for their work. We assign them a specific project to complete."

Four Directions bowl by Vince Bomberry, an Iroquoian artist. The *Four Directions* is an important concept in First Nations thinking. Each direction is associated with certain seasons, values, and philosophies. This museum exhibit explains what the symbolism means and why it was used.

Always something new

Melanie is constantly learning. "It's one of the best parts of my job," she says. "I have to become an expert in many different areas." To put together an exhibit, Melanie must study each item and the time period it is from. "You learn a lot about many different time periods in the past."

Activity

Make your own exhibit!

Put together a museum display yourself! It could be about your school, an interesting building, a particular shopping area, or even the community itself. As the museum coordinator, it is your job to present your subject so that others will know what is important about it.

First, you need to find out about your subject's past. You can do this by talking to people in the area, particularly older people who have lived there for a long time. What do they remember? Do they have any pictures? Check your local library. Ask the librarian for newspaper articles or books about your subject.

You need to collect objects. These might be old photographs, trophies or awards, yearbooks, or anything else that shows the story you want to tell.

When you have collected your materials, assemble them in a display. If you're not sure how to start, ask yourself these questions:
1. Is this school (or building or bridge or town) famous for anything?
2. How long has it been here?
3. Why was it built in that spot at that time?

Once you have decided on your display, find a place to show it. If you have chosen a public building, ask if you can display your work there. If you have chosen an old structure in your community, ask if you can show your exhibit in your school or local library.

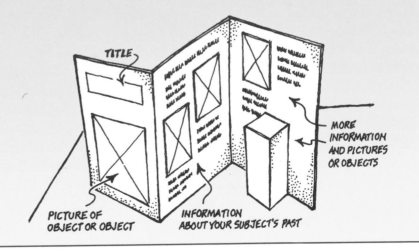

TITLE

MORE INFORMATION AND PICTURES OR OBJECTS

PICTURE OF OBJECT OR OBJECT

INFORMATION ABOUT YOUR SUBJECT'S PAST

How to become a museum coordinator

Melanie began her work with the museum while she was still in school. "I was a tour guide first, then a teacher in the education department."

Later, she applied for and received a Museum Studies internship for a year, to study how the museum worked. By this time she had also completed a Bachelor's degree in Physical Anthropology. Her first job with the museum was as a program coordinator.

Lots of choices

"It doesn't really matter what you study at the high school level: history, science, art, all of them have a place at a large museum. There are so many different jobs in the building. We have people working here with university degrees in ancient cultures, mammals, birds,

Much of a museum coordinator's time is spent keeping the exhibits in one piece. Here, a staff member wires together a suit of armor.

history, sculpture, and painting. A degree in Museum Studies is another way to enter this field."

Melanie adds that it is very difficult for anyone to get a job at the museum without a Bachelor's degree. "There is a lot of competition."

Hard work... and fun!

In this field, the amount of time you have to devote to your job varies. "I love my work so much that I have no personal life," Melanie laughs.

"I have made the museum my life, but you can do a lot or a little in this field. This job gives you lots of opportunities. I have done freelance work for other museums and art galleries because of what I do here."

Is this career for you?

Many people love museums and want to work in them. Consequently, there is always competition.

"I wish I'd figured it out earlier in my career. In this field, you have to start making contacts while you are still in school. I try to counsel the students: Make the contacts now, offer to do things, volunteer. Here at the museum, they rarely hire anyone they don't know. They don't have to. There is so much competition for the jobs that you have to have the credentials *and* be a familiar, hard-working, reliable face."

Melanie says all the hard work is worth it. "It's a wonderful job because you are always learning. It is never dull. No two days are ever the same.

"I have the best job in the museum. Our schedule here isn't rigid and we are never doing the same thing all day.

Melanie spends a great deal of time working with other people. She coordinates a group of 60 volunteers who help guide visitors, assemble displays, and provide help wherever they can. She needs good management skills to make sure everything gets done and everyone gets along.

Our work is diverse. We're not teaching or doing research or repairing the collection all day. We do a bit of everything. We are also independent. We have a lot of leeway in what we do. We can be as creative as we want to be. It is one of the best parts of the job."

Career planning

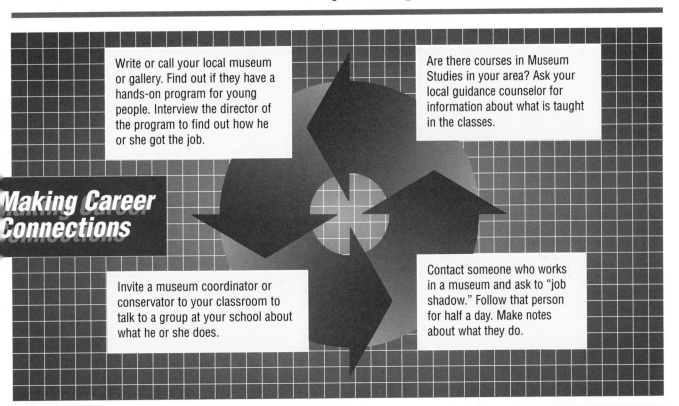

Write or call your local museum or gallery. Find out if they have a hands-on program for young people. Interview the director of the program to find out how he or she got the job.

Are there courses in Museum Studies in your area? Ask your local guidance counselor for information about what is taught in the classes.

Making Career Connections

Invite a museum coordinator or conservator to your classroom to talk to a group at your school about what he or she does.

Contact someone who works in a museum and ask to "job shadow." Follow that person for half a day. Make notes about what they do.

Getting started

Interested in working in a museum? Here's what you can do now.

1. Volunteer to work at a local museum. Many teenage volunteers help out with younger visitors and help lead creative arts programs.
2. Take a wide variety of courses in school. Be sure to include courses in both the arts and sciences. Don't forget the computer classes!
3. Find out as much as you can about museums around the world. You will learn many ways to present the past.
4. Coordinators need to know how to organize people, information, and money. Volunteer to work on committees at your school. Learn how to plan a dance or assembly.
5. Talk to the museum director or coordinator at your local museum. Ask if they have co-op positions.

Related careers

Here are some related careers you may want to check out.

Conservator
Repairs articles: Paintings, textiles, birds, mummies, books, to name a few. Must have patience and perseverance to work slowly and carefully with articles that are often very fragile.

Design artist
Designs and assembles the presentation of pieces for a museum display. Must have a good eye for balance and the knowledge to place historical or natural history items in the correct setting.

Teacher
Most teachers work in a school, but there are regular teachers in museums as well. They organize educational programs for schools and the general public. They need good communication skills and the ability to be at ease in front of large groups.

Future watch

Museums are changing. Computer technology is making new kinds of displays possible. Virtual reality equipment may soon produce a simulated Amazon jungle or medieval castle for visitors to explore. Computer databases will make much more background information available. Museums will require many people with lots of different skills to maintain the collections and create new ways to explore the past.

Jon Jouppien

Heritage Resource Consultant

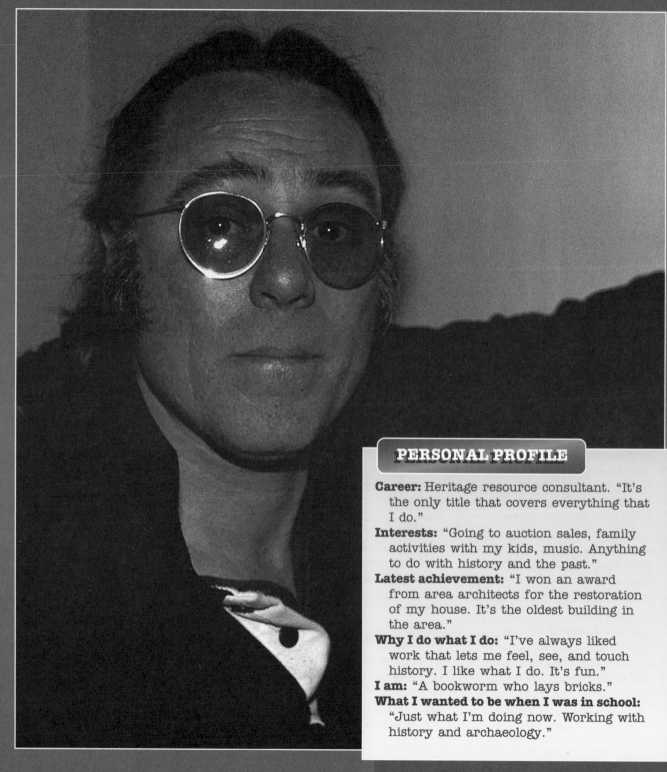

PERSONAL PROFILE

Career: Heritage resource consultant. "It's the only title that covers everything that I do."

Interests: "Going to auction sales, family activities with my kids, music. Anything to do with history and the past."

Latest achievement: "I won an award from area architects for the restoration of my house. It's the oldest building in the area."

Why I do what I do: "I've always liked work that lets me feel, see, and touch history. I like what I do. It's fun."

I am: "A bookworm who lays bricks."

What I wanted to be when I was in school: "Just what I'm doing now. Working with history and archaeology."

What a heritage resource consultant does

Jon Jouppien calls himself a self-employed "heritage resource consultant." He runs a small business, hiring out himself and his employees to do whatever jobs interest him. He works with the past and with old things in many different ways: as an archaeologist, as a builder, and as a museum advisor.

Digging up the past

When Jon works as an archaeologist, he and his crew dig up land where people once lived. They do this to try to discover how these people lived, what kinds of tools they used, and what their customs were.

"We might find two thousand artifacts when we dig up the site," Jon says. "Artifacts can be tools, kitchen utensils, building material — all sorts of things. We take them back to the office and clean them. Then we figure out what they are and what they can tell us about the history of the site. Then I write a report on what we've learned."

Replicating historical objects

Unfortunately, many objects that our ancestors used in everyday life have not survived. Materials such as paper and leather usually don't last for hundreds of years. When a museum wants to put together an exhibit, they often have to make replicas (reproductions) of certain items that just aren't around any more. Jon and his crew often do this sort of work. They make the needed items in the same way that they were made originally.

Rebuilding the past

Jon also works as a consultant, advising people how to renovate and restore old buildings. Jon and his crew may also do the actual work. "We may be asked to build just about anything," he grins. "It's good that my team has skills in all the major construction areas — plumbing, carpentry, masonry. They also know how those skills were used in the past. This helps make the restoration as authentic as possible."

Sometimes, other buildings were on the site and have since been torn down. Or, people built additions on the house over the centuries. "We figure out what used to be there, and what the house looked like when it was built. Then we try to replicate it as best we can." Jon smiles. "If it looks and feels the way it did when first built, then we've done our job well."

Displaying the past

The third part of Jon's work is setting up museum displays that depict the past. His team does everything, from building the actual display cases to advising the museum what to put in them. "We also find people who know how to reproduce the articles from the past that we need to complete our display."

Simeon Marcano is one of only a few cobblers who knows how to make shoes and boots the old-fashioned way, using wooden pegs rather than glue. "Before 1850," says Simeon, "shoes and boots were not made with a right and a left. The cobbler carved a wooden "last" (a model), and made two identical shoes. You gradually 'wore in' the shoes until they fit your feet."

All in a day's work

"I do so many different things that my days are never quite the same," Jon chuckles. One thing he does do every day is talk to people.

Doing an archeological survey

Sometimes, Jon has to deal with someone, such as a land developer, who may not be happy to be talking to him. "Any developer of raw land — land with no existing buildings — has to ensure that there are no historical artifacts on the site that might be destroyed by new construction." Government employees review the development plan and determine what needs to be done before the developer can build. Often, developers learn that they need to have an archaeological survey. "That makes them unhappy, because a survey slows down the building process and costs the developer money.

"A developer who needs a survey phones me and asks me to do it," continues Jon. "But the developer wants the survey done today and a report tomorrow! I have to explain that surveys can take about two months to do."

Once Jon has agreed to do the survey, he and his crew go to the building site. First, they excavate several "test pits." If they don't find anything in the test pits, then it is likely that nothing else is on the rest of the site.

"If we do find something in the ground, the developer may have to stop development or arrange a

Rebuilding the past

Recently, Jon and his crew completely disassembled an early 19th-century house, moved it, and reassembled it at another site. The crew took the house apart carefully, labeling each piece. The pieces were moved to the new location and stored while the foundation was prepared, and then the house was rebuilt. If you look at the "before" and "after" photographs, you can see that the second-floor windows have been removed. They were an addition — not part of the original construction — so they were taken out.

Jon and his crew built a temporary shelter to protect the pieces of house from the weather.

The house before it was moved (the "before" photo).

This fireplace mantle was just one of many fixtures stored inside the shelter while the house was being rebuilt.

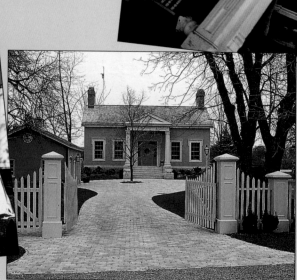

The house, rebuilt on its new site (the "after" photo).

more extensive survey." Jon must report back to the government and say what he finds. "Sometimes, what I have to say is not what the developer wants to hear. But I have to be honest to do a good job."

Saving an island

Sometimes Jon is called in to help save information in an area being changed by another "developer" — nature. "Recently, we got a call from the government. An eight-thousand-year-old burial site on an island was eroding, and the artifacts were in danger of being washed away by the river. We went out to record the site. We also did a survey of the rest of the island's shoreline and recorded all the other archaeological sites that were eroding." They found many artifacts, such as pieces of pottery and handmade nails. "There

was even a fur trader's ax from the 17th century," Jon exclaims. "It was just lying on the ground."

Jon recommended that the shoreline of the island be "stabilized" to stop it eroding. He suggested that government engineers build a seawall, but the engineers didn't agree. They wanted to plant willow trees to protect the shoreline. "We showed them photos of willow trees falling into the

river. Willow trees weren't going to save the island."

Unfortunately, the government did not have enough money to do anything to the island, and the shoreline continues to erode. "That's the frustration of what we do. You can only make recommendations. Without public interest in a site, nothing happens."

Running a business

In between working with a lot of interesting history, Jon spends part of each day running his business. "A big part of that job is paperwork," he complains. "I don't enjoy it, but I have to do it to keep my business running smoothly."

Here Jon puts the finishing touches on a museum display, depicting a room in the "colonial" era (about 200 years ago).

Activity

Restoration in action

Jon and his crew spend a lot of time repairing and fixing old things. You can practice some of the skills they use by giving an old toy a new life.

You will need
- old wooden toys (broken or in need of "sprucing up")
- arts and crafts supplies
- woodworking tools (if necessary)
- glue gun and glue

Procedure
1. Work on your own or with a group of friends. Examine each toy

carefully. Decide what repairs you need to do in order to restore the toy to "like-new" condition. You can find pictures of the toys, when new, in library books or department store catalogues, or by checking toy stores.
2. Do the restorations. Start by thoroughly cleaning each toy. Decide the order of repair. For example, should a piece be painted before or after it is glued back in place?
3. When you have finished restoring the toys, you could donate them to

Challenge

Display your restored toys in your library or school. Offer to do similar work for other people. You may have just started a new business!

a local school or day care. (Check that they are safe for the children — some older toys contained hazards.) Or have a craft sale and donate the money to a charity.

How to become a heritage resource consultant

"Start right away!" is Jon's advice to anyone who is interested in this field. "Don't let anyone tell you that you have to wait until you finish school. Pick something that interests you — houses, cars, gardening, carpentry — and start learning about it now." Jon recommends doing volunteer work on an historical site. "Any experience you can offer to an employer is valuable. Everything you do can help you later on."

Although Jon has a degree in archaeology as well as other training, he feels that a degree is not necessary for this business. "Several people on my team took post-secondary training in the building trades," he explains. "In fact, the broader your technical background, the better. It's great if you know how to do carpentry and wiring, but it's better if you also know how to make drawings and how to use a library or a computer to find information."

To help you run a business, Jon encourages you to learn basic skills. "And develop business sense," he adds. "Learn how to keep a budget and balance a bank account. Know how to use a computer — all these things you can learn to do right now."

Any skill in the construction trades can help to give you a start in the renovation business.

Is this career for you?

Jon says his job has only a few problems. One problem is the time it takes away from being with his family. "Running a small business does eat into your family time. The job itself is time-consuming enough. Then I have to spend hours doing the paperwork, ordering supplies, and keeping the account books up to date."

The job is also physically demanding at times. Jon cautions that you have to be physically fit and agile to do the work. "Also, we work with old-fashioned building materials, and some of them aren't as safe as today's materials. For example, the old kinds of mortars can burn your skin. Old paints often contain lead, which is toxic. So when we scrape off old paint, we wear masks and make sure we have good ventilation."

The job has other hazards as well. Old buildings are not always stable and it is easy to trip and fall. "One time, the whole crew came down with poison ivy. Another time, we were in the bush, surveying, and some hunters shot at us. They thought we were deer.

"But I wouldn't do anything different," Jon adds, "I love my work."

Jon's business sign is similar to an 18th-century tavern sign. Back then, people went to the taverns to learn what was happening in the community.

J.K. JOUPPIEN
HERITAGE RESOURCE CONSULTANT

Career planning

Ask permission to tour a building that is being renovated. Take photographs of the alterations that are being done. Research the history of the building, and make a poster showing the old building and how it is being renovated.

Call the anthropology department at a local post-secondary school and ask if there are any archaeological sites in your area. Ask if the archaeologist will let you visit the site.

Making Career Connections

Call your local museum and ask to job shadow the person who sets up displays. Make notes of the different tasks that the job involves.

Write to the nearest government office that deals with building restoration. (Your librarian can help you find the address.) Ask for a list of historical sites in your area. Find out how a building comes to be classified as a historical site.

Getting started

Interested in being a heritage resource consultant? Here's what you can do now.

1. Join the local historical society and volunteer to help on a historic renovation project.
2. Take math, science, and computer classes in school. All are useful, either in running a consulting business or in figuring out the best way to rebuild a building.
3. Read magazines and books about old buildings and how they were built.
4. Learn one or more of the construction skills that Jon and his crew use every day. Most schools have classes in carpentry, metalwork, sewing, and other important skills.
5. Visit museums to see what types of articles were used in everyday life in the past.

Related careers

Here are some related careers you may want to check out.

Architect
Designs and prepares working plans for new buildings, from small homes to huge office complexes. May also design and plan the renovation of old buildings.

Carpenter
Uses wood and other products to construct the framing of a building or make a piece of furniture. May do "finish" work, trimming doors and making cabinets for kitchens and bathrooms.

Mason
Builds fireplaces, walls, foundations, etc., from brick, concrete, stone, and other masonry products. Cleans and repairs the masonry on old buildings.

Structural engineer
Examines old buildings to make sure they are stable. Recommends ways to strengthen unstable buildings so they can be used again.

Future watch

These days, many people are much more aware of the need to preserve our cultural heritage. This has resulted in more government regulations that require developers to protect the historic information at their sites. This means a growing need for archaeologists and historical renovators. Computer skills and new technology will help these people catalogue and study historical artifacts, and compare them with similar artifacts from around the world.

Jennifer Dunn

Petroleum Geologist

PERSONAL PROFILE

Career: Petroleum geologist. "I'm an explorer, searching for oil and natural gas."

Interests: Environmental issues, hiking, biking, scuba diving. "I like just about any outdoor activity."

Latest accomplishment: "Finding a job doing what I love! I'm one of only five people in the exploration unit."

Why I do what I do: "I do this because I'm interested in it. I took a lot of different courses, but liked geology best. The job is great because I use my skills constantly. It's never dull."

I am: Adventurous, a thrill-seeker, not concerned with "fitting in." "I do what makes me happy."

What I wanted to be when I was in school: "Jane Goodall! I always wanted to be a scientist of some kind. I wanted to be on the cover of *National Geographic*."

What a petroleum geologist does

Geologists are scientists who study the Earth. They want to know what it was like in the past and how it has changed over time. They ask these questions: What kinds of materials make up a particular area of the planet? What caused them to be where they are? How have they changed over millions of years?

Petroleum geologists, like Jennifer Dunn, spend their time looking for oil and natural gas — two different forms of petroleum. "We use our knowledge of the Earth to find possible locations of oil and natural gas deposits," explains Jennifer. "Then we work with engineers and drilling rig operators to get the oil and gas out of the ground."

Figuring out what is there

"Geologists are often called 'rock hounds'," Jennifer says. "But most geologists don't get to look at too many rocks. Because rocks are deep underground, we gather data about them, analyze the data, and make maps."

Gathering data means using a variety of tests to examine the Earth's characteristics. Jennifer might need to find out, for example, what kind of rock is at a particular location. "Since the rock might be deep down, I can't actually look at what I want to see."

She draws maps based on her tests. These maps show what she thinks an area is like, deep below the surface. The company she works for uses these maps to find different things: water, minerals, or fossil fuels (like oil and natural gas).

Tests

Scientific tests and specialized tools allow geologists to figure out what substances make up the rock below the surface. When they know that, they can determine whether there might be oil or natural gas in the rock.

"For example, we may use a gamma-ray detector to measure the natural radiation in a drill hole," explains Jennifer. "Certain minerals, such as clays, are more radioactive than others. Clays are not likely to contain oil. This is because they are not porous — there are few spaces within them where oil could move. So if the detector shows high natural radioactivity, that area is probably not a good place to drill for oil."

Protecting the environment

Jennifer is concerned about the environment as well as finding natural gas. She and her co-workers design ways to protect and preserve the environment around any drill site. "We're responsible for the site for a long time, not just for today," explains Jennifer. "We have to make sure that the area is reclaimable after the company leaves. That means we have to restore the original landscape within a certain amount of time depending on regulations. We often replant full-grown trees or restore wetlands." This process can be very costly, so her company preserves as much of the natural landscape as possible, before drilling begins.

Oil and dinosaurs do mix!

Oil and natural gas are usually found in sedimentary rock — layered rock that was made from small pieces of other rock. Fossils like this dinosaur bone are also found in sedimentary rock. The black circle next to the bone is a camera lens cover, to show the size of the bone

All in a day's work

On some days, Jennifer goes to "the field." This means that she goes to look at rocks, and tries to understand what they can tell her.

"We use a special drill to take a plug of rock, called a 'core sample,' out of the ground. We study the core to see what it can tell us about how that rock was formed and whether oil might be contained in it.

Ammonites: A geologist's time clock

This large fossil is an ammonite, a squid-like animal with a curved shell. For millions of years, each new layer of sediment that was deposited on the ocean floor contained the shells of ammonites. Noticeable changes in their shells happened at least every 300 000 years (a very short time by geological standards.) By studying the types of ammonites found in a particular rock, they can determine the age of that rock.

Paleontologist Cam Tsujita with a cast made from a giant ammonite fossil. Most ammonites are not this large.

Office work

On other days, Jennifer works at her office drafting table, examining and analyzing the data from the tests. "I spend a lot of my time trying to figure out what could be underground," she explains. "My analysis is based on the nature of the rocks and what we know about the surrounding area."

One of the most exciting parts of Jennifer's job is making a presentation about her findings. "I don't do this until I pull all the data together. First I show my data to an engineer. The engineer calculates the probability of finding oil, using a type of mathematics called statistics.

As a team, we can then present our work to our manager." Jennifer may tell her manager that there is, for example, an 85 percent probability of finding oil or gas at that site. Based on her recommendations, the company then has to decide whether or not to invest the money in drilling.

This is the part of the drilling rig that does the actual drilling. Why do you think it is called a "Christmas tree?"

A drilling rig. The Christmas tree is just to the right of the little house, below the large pulley or "block."

Site work

After the company has decided to drill in a certain place, Jennifer visits the drilling site. Petroleum geologists are responsible for keeping an eye on the drilling. "This part of the job requires feedback from the drilling team. We check the cores and tests as the drill goes deeper. Are we finding what was expected? If we aren't, we have to decide whether to continue or to try another site. Was the data analysis wrong? Is the drilling wrong? It can

be tough to decide because we're working way down in the Earth's crust.

"When they start drilling, that's when I cross my fingers. It's an exciting time!"

After oil is found, the drillers take the drilling rig apart and take it away. Then they install a pump, like this one, which continuously pumps the oil into a pipeline.

It's a Fact

Oil is still being formed beneath the Earth's surface. However, much of what we use today was formed before the dinosaurs walked the Earth.

Activity

How old is old? Making a timeline

The Earth is very old. In fact, "geological time" is measured in millions of years. The events and dates listed here show how long ago certain events occurred. Seeing these dates stretched out on a timeline is a great way to understand how old "old" really is.

You will need

- string, a little more than 5 m long
- colored markers or pens
- labels with adhesive on one side, tags, or paper and glue
- a ruler or measuring tape

Procedure

1. Tie each end of the string to something solid about 5 m apart. One end represents when the Earth was formed, the other end represents "today."
2. Starting at one end, make 1 m of string represent a billion (1 000 000 000) years. Divide your string into billion-year segments, and mark each segment on the string with a

marker. How many years does 1 cm represent?
3. Write each date and event listed below on a label.
4. Attach the labels to the string making the timeline "proportional." This means that each event should be placed on the string according to how long ago it occurred.

Sit back and look at your timeline. What do you see?
- How long have humans been on Earth compared with dinosaurs?

Challenge

How could you use your timeline to demonstrate the difference between the amount of time humans have lived on Earth and the time dinosaurs lived?

- How long did the Earth exist before animal life began?
- How long did the dinosaurs live?
- What other events fall between the dates you tracked?

Event	Number of years ago
Formation of the Earth	4 600 000 000
First evidence of life	3 800 000 000
First fish	500 000 000
First land animals	350 000 000
First dinosaurs	225 000 000
First birds	150 000 000
Extinction of the dinosaurs	65 000 000
First humans	2 000 000
End of the last Ice Age	11 000
Building of the Egyptian Pyramids	4 500
Year "zero" on modern calendar	2 000

How to become a petroleum geologist

Most geologists begin their work by taking geology courses after finishing high school. "There are college courses and technical courses," notes Jennifer. "You can usually get site-work with a technical school diploma."

Jennifer took a lot of science and math in high school. "If your high school doesn't offer geology courses, start out with general science — chemistry, physics, biology, and geography." Jennifer says you don't have to be brilliant in all areas of science to succeed. "You need a basic understanding of physics and calculus. I struggled with these throughout school."

Getting a job in geology

"The easiest and quickest way to get a permanent job is to get a summer job with an oil company. Then work very hard — work yourself into the ground!" Jennifer spent each summer during her post-secondary studies working in some aspect of geology. Few of the jobs were glamorous.

"I spent one summer mapping for the government," Jennifer recalls, "walking around figuring out where the different types of rocks were. It was a difficult job, made even worse by blackflies."

Geologists often travel to interesting places. Jennifer spent one summer studying coral reefs near Zanzibar Island, off the east coast of Africa.

Is this career for you?

"If you hate getting dirty, don't take this job," advises Jennifer. "Being a petroleum geologist is not the cleanest job around. Most geologists wear jeans and boots in the field. They are outdoorsy people, and spend at least one or two months a year in the field."

One advantage is the opportunity to travel. "Most geologists like the kind of life that takes them to interesting places. You can end up almost anywhere in the world." Jennifer has spent her summers working in northern and western Canada, Indonesia, and Zanzibar.

Travel and field work can be combined with having a family. "Usually you can take your kids with you. A lot of field work is done in the summer, because that's the best time to do it. Your kids can have really great summer vacations in interesting places."

Jennifer recommends that if you are interested in geology, you should take an introductory course that involves field work. "You work eighteen-hour days and it is physically demanding. But if you like this sort of work, geology may be just the career for you."

Many people find good jobs doing the physical work at a drilling site. This man wears a safety harness because he works at the top of the drilling rig.

Career planning

Go to a natural history museum and visit the dinosaur and geology exhibits. Many fossils were formed at the same time as oil and natural gas.

Contact both a university and a technical training institute and request information on their programs in geology. (You may be able to find this information on the Internet.) Compare how much training and time each requires.

Making Career Connections

Sign up for a co-op program that will allow you to work in a lab or as a field assistant in one of the sciences.

Ask permission to job shadow a geologist at work. You can find one by calling your local water department or any petroleum or mining company. Make notes and take photographs of the different parts of the job.

Getting started

Interested in being a petroleum geologist? Here's what you can do now.

1. Take as many science and math classes as you can.
2. Take a course in orienteering. Although not required for geologists or site workers, it is useful when you are working in the field.
3. Learn first-aid. It may come in handy when you are working far away from modern medical facilities.
4. Talk to area farmers or ranchers. Find out how the type of soil in your area affects how local people live and work.
5. Join a science club at school. Practice giving presentations of scientific data to other members of the club.
6. Ask your school guidance counselor for ideas on summer jobs in science and geology.

Related careers

Here are some related careers you may want to check out.

Paleontologist
Researches fossils of plants and animals. Describes ancient forms of life, and prepares timelines showing when each form inhabited the Earth.

Geochemist
Determines the chemical properties of minerals. Combines chemistry and geology to figure out the prehistoric climate and environment of an area.

Geologic technician
Collects core samples, analyzes data from tests, and other rock samples and does surveying work for a geologist. Usually requires a two-year diploma course from a college or technical training school.

Drill rig operator
Manages the drilling equipment on the drill site. Must understand mechanics and how to repair the equipment.

Future watch

"Geologists are now exploring under the oceans and in the Arctic," Jennifer notes. "There are many places left to search for oil and gas." Scientists will also have to find different ways to meet humanity's energy needs. This search continues with the exploring of new uses of nuclear and solar forms of energy. Another direction for a geology career is to become more involved with caring for the Earth. Geologists will need to become experts in using Earth's resources wisely and carefully.

Andrew Devai

Comic Store Manager

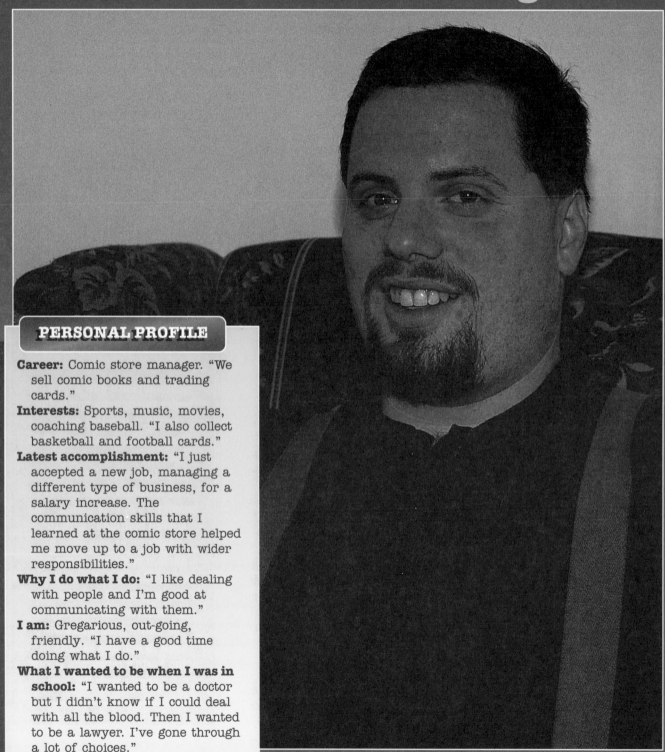

PERSONAL PROFILE

Career: Comic store manager. "We sell comic books and trading cards."

Interests: Sports, music, movies, coaching baseball. "I also collect basketball and football cards."

Latest accomplishment: "I just accepted a new job, managing a different type of business, for a salary increase. The communication skills that I learned at the comic store helped me move up to a job with wider responsibilities."

Why I do what I do: "I like dealing with people and I'm good at communicating with them."

I am: Gregarious, out-going, friendly. "I have a good time doing what I do."

What I wanted to be when I was in school: "I wanted to be a doctor but I didn't know if I could deal with all the blood. Then I wanted to be a lawyer. I've gone through a lot of choices."

What a comic store manager does

Andrew Devai works for a small family-owned business called *The Comic Connection.* He sells new and collectible comic books, sports cards, and several other popular collectible items. There are eight employees but only three of them are full-time. "During the week, just the three of us — the owners Ted and Brenda, and me — run the store."

Because the staff is so small, Andrew does a little bit of everything. "That's what's nice about a small business," he notes. "The job description is that you do what needs to be done: ordering, shipping, selling, and office work."

What's it worth?

An important part of Andrew's job is pricing merchandise. In a store that has thousands of different books and cards for sale, that's a big job. Andrew uses price guides to give him an idea of what each item is worth. "If I charge more for a card or comic than the price quoted in the book, the customers won't buy it."

If the price is too low, the store may lose money on the sale or it may not sell for another reason. "Oddly enough," Andrew recalls, "a low price can scare customers away! We had one card — a Patrick Roy rookie card — that Ted got for a very good price. He decided to pass on his savings, and priced the card unusually low. However, this card was very popular, and everyone knew what it was worth. When they saw the price, the first thing they asked was 'What's wrong with it?'!"

Dealing with customers

One of the most difficult things that Andrew does is buy old cards and comics from people who just walk into the store to sell them. "People have an idea that their property is worth a lot of money. Sometimes it is. Sometimes it isn't."

Andrew has to think about several things when he offers to buy a comic or card. First, the item has to be in very good condition. Second, there has to be a demand for it. "Somebody else has to want it or we won't be able to sell it." Third, Andrew and the person selling the card must agree on a price. "Sometimes people won't budge on the price. But I have to figure out how much we could sell it for before I make an offer to buy it."

Work is fun!

Andrew says one of the best parts of working for *The Comic Connection* is getting to handle something he likes collecting.

Rookie cards of top players become very valuable. This rookie card of hockey star Wayne Gretsky is worth over $900.

Sometimes comics become valuable even before they're very old. This one — Spawn — quadrupled in value in just six months.

All in a day's work

The store is open from 10:00 a.m. to 8:00 p.m. Andrew alternates "shifts" with Ted, working either a 10-6 or 12-8 shift. "Mornings are always slower," he explains, "so the person on the 10-6 shift opens things up and sets out any merchandise. There is always something to do. Pricing and sorting cards or comics takes up a lot of time."

Working odd hours

Being a store manager means working some nights and weekends. "It takes me about three nights to prepare the order for new comic books. We estimate how many we'll sell, and hope that we haven't ordered too many or too few. I use a

computer now so it takes less time to make up the order."

Every Tuesday afternoon, new comic books arrive. Everything must be counted. Then the books for regular subscribers are distributed into the store's mailboxes in the back room. Andrew says it takes about two hours to do this, without any interruptions. "But I always have interruptions!" he chuckles.

The customer is always right

Dealing with customers is a big part of Andrew's job every day. "They can be a lot of fun or they

Andrew has to know how valuable a card is before he can put a price on it to sell to the public.

How old is old?

"Old" can mean a lot of different ages, depending on what you're talking about. At The Comic Connection, "old" is usually some time in the first half of the 20th century. Although the first comic book appeared in 1897, Andrew says they weren't like what we see today. The first comic book that looks like today's comics was called *Funnies on Parade* and was published in 1933. Many of today's superheros first appeared in North American comics during the years of World War II. These include Superman, Batman, The Flash, Daredevil, Aquaman, and Wonder Woman.

The first sports cards were given free in packages of cigarettes. They appeared in 1887 and showed pictures of baseball players, boxers, and wrestlers. Hockey cards appeared in the 1910s. In the 1920s, candy manufacturers packaged baseball cards with their products. Back then, a flat piece of bubble gum with five cards cost one cent.

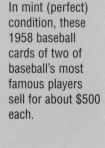

In mint (perfect) condition, these 1958 baseball cards of two of baseball's most famous players sell for about $500 each.

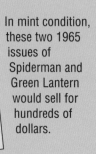

In mint condition, these two 1965 issues of Spiderman and Green Lantern would sell for hundreds of dollars.

When they get a chance, the store's owner and employees try out new merchandise. Here they're playing a game of Magic, The Gathering, one of the first collectible card games.

can be supremely frustrating," laughs Andrew. "But most of them are great."

A lot of young collectors come into the store, wanting to fill out their sports card sets. "Ted came up with the idea of keeping notebooks filled with individually priced cards. But the kids can get caught up in all that's available. They used to pull huge piles of cards out of the books, far more than they could afford to buy. Now, I ask them up front 'How much money do you have to spend?' Then I help them pick out what they can afford. Patience helps in this situation."

The ups and downs of a small business

"The worst day I had on the job was December 24, three years ago," Andrew recalls somberly. "We came to work and the store had been robbed. It's pretty traumatic when something like that happens.

"However, the best day I had on the job was one day when Ted and I were opening up a box of cards. Every so often, the manufacturer puts a really valuable card in a set. You can't tell it's there until after you buy the whole pack. I picked up the last pack and told Ted, 'It's the last pack. I'll bet I find something.' I opened it and there was a special Shaquille O'Neal card. It was probably worth about $300."

Activity

Learning about the past from your collection

Collections of historical objects such as stamps, coins, dolls, tools, sports cards, bottles, and spoons can tell us about the past. Select items from your own collection, or from the collection of a friend or relative and use them to produce a display.

You will need
  poster-size piece of bristol board
  tape or glue
  markers or pens
  5 - 10 items from your collection

Procedure
1. Find out what year your items were made. This will probably require a trip to your school (or local) library. An encyclopedia is a good place to start.

2. Once you know approximately when each item was made, find out what was happening then. What events were important in the news? For example, if you collect old political campaign buttons, you might choose to find out what issues were important in that campaign.

3. Make a poster showing what happened in the year each of your items was made. Mount small items on the poster. Number the larger items, and display them along with the poster.

4. Ask your history or social studies teacher if you may use the poster as a project.

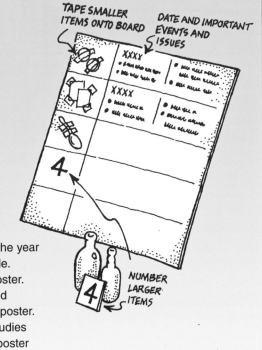

TAPE SMALLER ITEMS ONTO BOARD

DATE AND IMPORTANT EVENTS AND ISSUES

NUMBER LARGER ITEMS

How to become a comic store manager

"I got into this business by accident," Andrew recalls. "I wasn't happy with my old job, and my friend Ted was losing one of his staff members. He asked me if I wanted to manage a store for him. The original idea was that I would be managing a second store. But the economy went into a recession, so we didn't expand and I'm here in the main store."

Know your product

"The main thing about running a small business is that you really have to know what you're selling. It doesn't matter if it's cards or comics or cars, the more you know about your product, the better off you'll be."

Andrew says that education is always important. Store managers need to learn business and communication skills. "A lot of high school and tech school programs will teach you about running a small business." Accounting skills are useful, but Andrew emphasizes that communication skills are even more important. "Running a small business is dealing with people and communicating with them. You are always dealing with the public. That's what this business is."

Andrew adds that a knowledge of current events also comes in handy. "If you know what's going on in the world around you, you adjust the business accordingly. If the economy

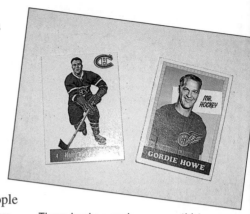

These hockey cards are over thirty years old.

is bad in your area, you don't invest in as much stock. It makes sense that if people in your area are out of work, they won't be able to buy non-essential things such as comics."

Is this career for you?

Andrew advises anyone who wants to go into this kind of business to know the market. "Some customers, especially trading card and comic book customers, try to barter for lower prices! So, you also have to know how to bargain. Try to be consistent in the way you deal with all your customers.

"If you're running your own business, you give up a lot of your freedom. You have to plan to do whatever needs to be done. We're open seven days a week and somebody has to be here. If you're the manager, that's your job."

Andrew adds that if you're well-organized, you don't have to have extra long days every day. "You do have free time if you use your time on the job well." He smiles and holds up a card. "And I enjoy my time at work, too!"

Helping customers is part of Andrew's job. Here he and a customer track down a card to complete a set.

Career planning

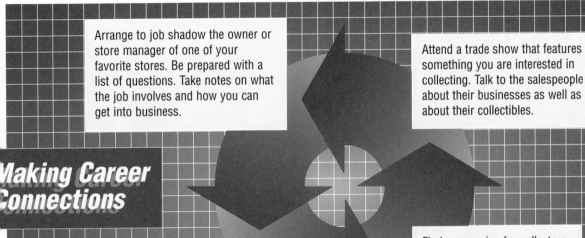

Arrange to job shadow the owner or store manager of one of your favorite stores. Be prepared with a list of questions. Take notes on what the job involves and how you can get into business.

Attend a trade show that features something you are interested in collecting. Talk to the salespeople about their businesses as well as about their collectibles.

Making Career Connections

Use the Internet or a local computer bulletin board service (BBS) to contact other collectors. Share information about "what's hot and what's not."

Find a magazine for collectors in the library. Examine the advertisements. Make a list of five types of businesses that advertise in that magazine.

Getting started

Interested in managing your own collectibles store? Here's what you can do now.

1. Know your product. Learn all you can about what you want to collect and eventually sell.
2. Visit a museum and examine the different ways that items are displayed. What information is provided about each item?
3. Take courses in math and computers. You will need the skills you learn to run your own business.
4. A small business owner has to learn to manage even when business is not good. Learn to budget your money.
5. Speak up! The best way to learn to talk with other people is by doing it. Courses in debating and public speaking can also help.
6. Apply for a job at a local store. Many salespeople start by working at a part-time job.

Related careers

Here are some related careers you may want to check out.

Coin and stamp dealer

Sells coins or stamps to collectors and investors. Must know the history of each piece and its current value.

Wholesaler

Buys goods in large amounts from manufacturers, and sells them in smaller amounts to retail stores. May import goods from other countries.

Graphic artist

Designs and draws artwork for comic books, trading cards, advertising material, signs, posters, etc. May work "freelance," working for many different clients.

Store manager

Manages the day-to-day selling of merchandise in a retail store. Depending on the size of the store, deals with employees and scheduling, customer inquiries, and ordering and delivery of merchandise.

Future watch

There will always be shops that cater to people's hobbies. These stores will need good salespeople who know and understand the hobby. Andrew says that his particular area is expanding. "There are more and better artists and writers moving into the field."

New methods of selling are also arising as the Internet — the electronic communications network — grows. On-line communication will make more products available over greater distances. Tomorrow's salespeople will have to understand how to use computers in many areas of their work.

Charlotte Dean

Set and Costume Designer

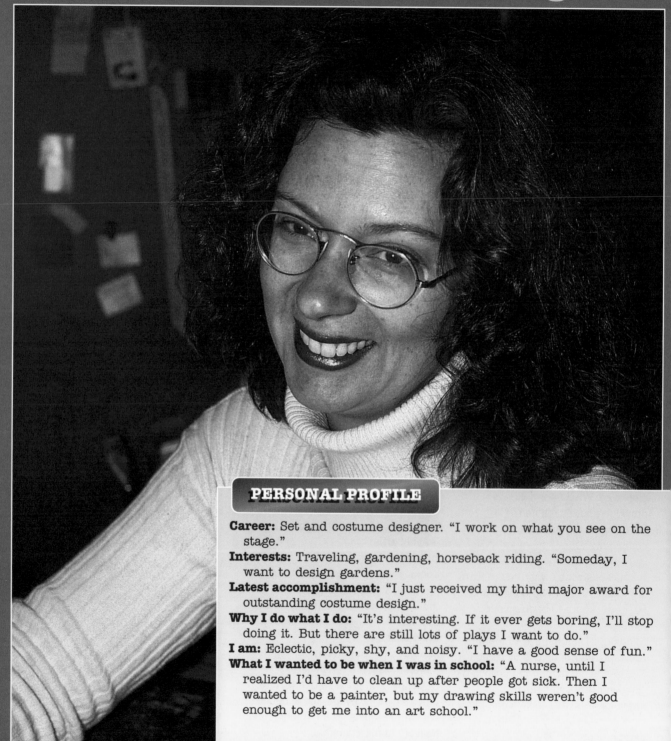

PERSONAL PROFILE

Career: Set and costume designer. "I work on what you see on the stage."

Interests: Traveling, gardening, horseback riding. "Someday, I want to design gardens."

Latest accomplishment: "I just received my third major award for outstanding costume design."

Why I do what I do: "It's interesting. If it ever gets boring, I'll stop doing it. But there are still lots of plays I want to do."

I am: Eclectic, picky, shy, and noisy. "I have a good sense of fun."

What I wanted to be when I was in school: "A nurse, until I realized I'd have to clean up after people got sick. Then I wanted to be a painter, but my drawing skills weren't good enough to get me into an art school."

What a set and costume designer does

Charlotte Dean designs what actors wear in a play and what sets and scenery will appear on the stage with them. "I'm responsible for the 'look' of a production," she says.

There is a lot more to creating this "look" than just sewing fabric and hammering nails. "I need to research the five Ws — who, what, when, where, why — before I decide how a play should look."

Detail makes a difference

Any play that portrays the past requires a lot of research. "I can't just use today's clothing and scenery," explains Charlotte. "I have to find out what life was like at the time of the play. For example, recently I worked on an 18th-century show. I found out that women of the aristocracy wore boned corsets and powdered wigs. My costumes had to include those things. But I couldn't dress a servant the same way that I dressed the duchess. The female servants wore simple dark-colored dresses and white aprons."

Charlotte likes to make the costumes historically accurate. When the play called for boned corsets, that's what the actors really wore. "But they complained that they were uncomfortable," laughs Charlotte. "So, we cheated a little by inserting a panel of stretchy fabric so they could breathe more easily."

Doing what the director orders

"One person, usually the director, is in charge of the whole production," notes Charlotte. "The designer is responsible to the director. I consult with the director to discuss how a show should look.

"The director is concerned with the effect that the play has on the audience," Charlotte adds. "What I use in my designs depends on what the director and the play are trying to do. If the director wants to stimulate the audience, I use bright jarring colors. If the play's goal is to make people uncomfortable, then I can use tricks with the sets to help do that.

"I also have to know if the show will be touring," comments Charlotte. "I don't want to design a set that is too complicated to take apart, move, and set up again."

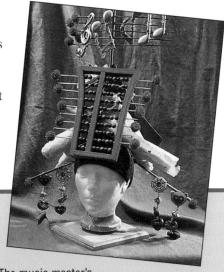

The music master's costume includes an ornate coat and a fantastic headdress made of styrofoam and shish-ka-bob skewers. Look closely at the picture and you'll see that the musical notes are attached to a school pointer just like the ones used in classrooms.

Costumes: From concept to opening night

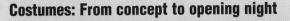

Charlotte spends a lot of time working on a show's costumes. The designs, like the one above from *The Nightingale*, start out as painted drawings with samples of fabric.

All in a day's work

"**F**irst," Charlotte says, "no two days are alike. I am usually working on more than one play at a time. Each play is in a different stage of development, but I do more or less the same things for each one."

All in a play's work

"When I'm offered a show to design, I analyze the script first. This is when I come up with some ideas of how the play should look on stage. Then I meet with the director, usually several times, to learn how he or she wants the show to look."

Charlotte's designs for each set requires many drawings, including floor plans, elevations, and backdrops. She attaches fabric samples to each costume sketch, and paints the colors she wants on the sketch. Carpenters and fabric cutters work from these drawings.

Charlotte's work doesn't stop once her drawings are approved. The next stage of her job is shopping. "This is great fun," she grins. "I find my materials in the places you might expect — fabric stores, interior decorating shops, antiques shops — and in some places you might not expect — plastics companies, estate and auction sales, hardware stores. I've even used corn husks out of a farmer's field."

Natural cotton or synthetic polyester?

Fabric is very important. Charlotte learned what works and what doesn't through experience. "People say that designers are sticklers for using natural fabrics. We are, but for a good reason. Under the hot lights, the actors get very warm. Natural fabrics breathe better and help them stay cool." Natural fabrics also absorb and reflect light better than artificial fabrics such as polyester. This makes them look more "real" on stage.

Once Charlotte and the director have agreed on designs and materials, Charlotte supervises the making of everything she has designed. That means working with cutters and sewers to make the

Hammers and nails

Developing a set goes through many stages. While designing the set, Charlotte draws plans or "blueprints," and makes a miniature model of it. Then, she must describe each detail to the carpenters who build the set.

Charlotte shows the carpenter the blueprint of the set she wants built, and discusses any possible problems.

This is the finished set with the lighting designer's work added.

costumes, and with carpenters and technicians to construct the sets.

Rehearsals are important

Charlotte attends several rehearsals as the play is prepared. At the first "read-through" rehearsal, she shows her sketches and concepts to the actors. The next important rehearsal for Charlotte is the "cue-to-cue" rehearsal. The actors walk through the play (without speaking all the lines) to make sure all the elements — such as sound

---

The actor who wears this dress must also wear a corset and a petticoat to make the skirt stand out properly.

and lighting — work. At this rehearsal, Charlotte gets a good idea of how her designs and those of the lighting designer suit each other.

Then comes the technical dress rehearsal or "tech dress." "This is the first time the actors wear the costumes on stage," Charlotte explains. "It's my chance to see what problems might crop up. Sometimes I find out that an actor has to change costume more quickly than I had thought. In that case, I build one costume to fit on top of another, and fasten it with a lot of velcro."

If there are no set or costume problems, most of Charlotte's job with the production is finished. She goes to the final dress rehearsal but rarely attends the play's opening. "Opening night is exciting, but by then I'm usually working on another play and my mind is elsewhere."

Activity

Figuring out the footwear

In the costumes Charlotte designs, the footwear provides the audience with a lot of information about each character. Do the shoes people wear every day give a message about who they are? Find out by conducting a survey.

You will need
- a camera and film
- poster board
- questionnaires and pens

Procedure
1. Find five people you know who work in different occupations. Ask if you may take their photographs.

2. Take photographs of the shoes each person normally wears to work.
3. Take a photograph of each person at work, without their feet in the picture!
4. Mount your pictures on a poster, all mixed up. Number the people pictures 1 to 5, and label the feet pictures A to E.
5. Show the poster to your friends and give them a questionnaire like the one shown here. Ask them to answer the questions.

Questionnaire:

1. Match the shoes with the occupation!

2. Can you tell anything else about the people from the shoes they are wearing?

3. Do the shoes tell you anything else? For example, what season is it? Where does each person live?

4. How many did your friends get right? Make a list of your friends' ideas about what shoes "say" about a person.

5. Start a design notebook with the pictures and your friends' reactions filed together. Keep this notebook for future reference on design projects.

How to become a set and costume designer

Charlotte began designing after earning a bachelor's degree in Fine Arts. However, she is quick to point out that you don't need a degree. "I'm glad I did," she notes, "but there are technical schools that will give you a good start. You can also start straight from high school."

Charlotte recommends several courses that have helped her in her work. "Math, for example. I need it for setting specifications on sets and costumes. Computer classes are also critical because a lot of design work is now done on computer. Any course dealing with the visual arts is helpful: drawing, painting, sculpture." Charlotte also recommends taking history classes. "You need as much information as possible to be able to imagine and recreate how a time in the past looked."

Learning the ropes

Charlotte advises young people who want to work in design to volunteer now to work in a theater. "It is great if you have a skill to offer, but at first you could simply volunteer to be a 'gofer' — the person who runs errands for the director. You could also offer to help design sets and costumes for school plays. Volunteer work and previous design experience is very valuable when you start applying for jobs." If you

have worked on a production, you may be taken on as an apprentice. "Apprentice time is important. Designers' ideas and techniques are handed down from one person to another."

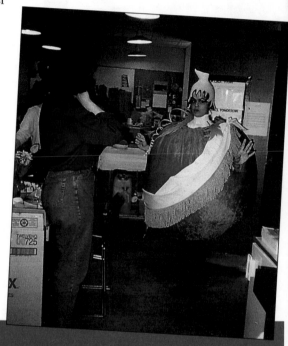

Not all of Charlotte's costumes are from the past. She designs whatever is needed, even a tomato!

Is this career for you?

Charlotte is a freelance designer. She sets her own hours and decides when she wants to work. When she works for someone as a designer, she signs a contract that states what she will do and how much they will pay her to do it. This can be a scary way to live. Although she usually has a lot of work, there are times when she doesn't know what she will be doing in six months.

"This business is very 'word-of-mouth.' Someone might give me a project based on what someone else said about my work in the past. It takes a while to build a reputation. Also, with so much funding being cut from government budgets, money is tighter. We go through hard times in the arts."

She also points out that the hours are not regular. "Once rehearsals start, you are at the beck and call of the production. You have to meet with people when they want you to be there. This means your personal life may need to be juggled."

Charlotte says she works between forty and a hundred hours a week. That seems like a lot but she says she wouldn't have it any other way. "Your time is your own and that's important. I have the advantage of being able to say 'I'm not going to work in July.'"

Charlotte sketches and paints her ideas for costumes and sets.

Career planning

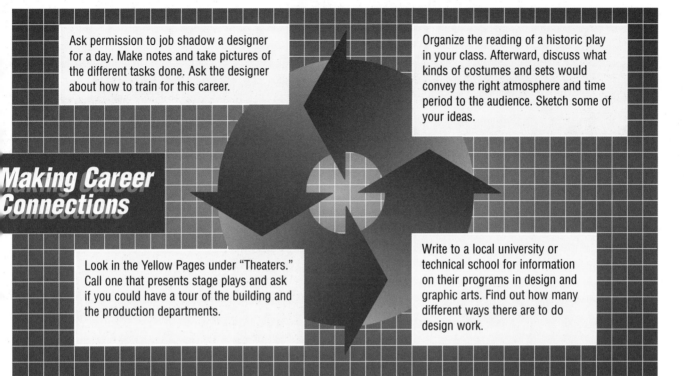

Making Career Connections

Ask permission to job shadow a designer for a day. Make notes and take pictures of the different tasks done. Ask the designer about how to train for this career.

Organize the reading of a historic play in your class. Afterward, discuss what kinds of costumes and sets would convey the right atmosphere and time period to the audience. Sketch some of your ideas.

Look in the Yellow Pages under "Theaters." Call one that presents stage plays and ask if you could have a tour of the building and the production departments.

Write to a local university or technical school for information on their programs in design and graphic arts. Find out how many different ways there are to do design work.

Getting started

Interested in being a set and costume designer? Here's what you can do now.

1. Volunteer to construct sets or make costumes at a local theater or for your school drama club. Keep photographs of your work so you will have them to show to future employers.
2. Start designing now. If costumes interest you, learn to sew. If sets appeal to you, take a course in woodworking or construction.
3. Take plenty of math and computer classes, plus art, history, and design at school.
4. Visit museums and art galleries and examine old costumes and furniture. Think about why certain objects make you feel a certain way.
5. Apply for a summer job at a historic site or theme park. Many students are hired to reenact scenes of daily life in the past.

Related careers

Here are some related careers you may want to check out.

Lighting designer
Designs the lighting for a play. Prepares a script to tell the lighting technicians which lights to use and when.

Director
Directs a play by combining many elements: actors, dialogue, costumes, sets, and lighting. Is responsible for how the play looks, feels, and affects the audience.

Fashion designer
Designs clothing to sell to the public. Does many of the same things that Charlotte does, but works with current trends and styles.

Wig maker
Constructs the wigs worn by actors in plays and movies. Uses both synthetic and human hair. Must know the different wig styles from the past.

Future watch

Computers are already having a great effect on the theater and will continue to change the way plays are constructed. Historical accuracy is improving because computers help us research information more easily. Computers also help in set design and construction. They make it possible to calculate very specific measurements. Designers also use computers to get an idea of the proportion and balance of a set before construction starts.

Richard Simonsen

Antique Car Restorer

PERSONAL PROFILE

Career: Antique car restorer. "I put cars back in the shape they started in."

Interests: "Painting and drawing, music, sailing. My wife and I have raced sailboats for twelve years."

Latest accomplishment: "I've just about finished restoring a beautiful and rare car: the 1930 Bentley Speed Six."

Why I do what I do: "I just like automobiles. I like making things. I'm sure I'd do the same thing whether or not I could make a living at it."

I am: Meticulous, precise, solitary. "I work alone every day, all day. I prefer it that way."

What I wanted to be when I was in school: "I've always loved cars but I had no desire to do restoration as a livelihood. I wanted to be a painter, an artist."

What an antique car restorer does

"It's a hobby gone wrong," says Richard Simonsen with a laugh. Richard restores old cars to new condition, something he's been interested in since he was a teenager. Now he makes his living restoring Bentleys and Bugattis, and an occasional Hispano Suiza, from the 1920s and 1930s.

"Back then," explains Richard, "you bought a chassis — a driveable unit without a body — from a dealer or manufacturer. They had different styles of bodies that you could choose. Once you chose the style you wanted, they took your chassis to a coach builder. The coach builder then completed the car. Many luxury-car manufacturers continued this tradition for many years. Rolls Royce didn't make their own bodywork until the 50s."

Tracking down an antique car

Those luxury-car manufacturers made only a small number of cars each year, and each one was different. To do a proper restoration, Richard has to figure out which one of these cars he is dealing with. "Fortunately," he says, "that's not too much of a problem. Two things help. First, the factories kept very good records of who owned each car and what kind of work was done to it. Second, most of these cars are from England, where the license plate stayed with the car even when it was sold. This helps me trace the car's history."

The cars Richard restores have been popular since they were first built. A lot of pictures of them still exist so he is usually able to find a picture of the exact car he is working on. Then the dirty work begins.

The driver's door without the upholstery panel. The door knob is added after the upholstery panel is attached.

What's underneath a Bentley

"Someone brought this Bentley over from England in 1950 disassembled. Someone in Pennsylvania bought it for parts to rebuild other Bentleys. What remained cost me about seven thousand dollars. Since only about 175 cars of this model were made, it's pretty rare. Finished, this car is worth about half a million dollars."

That's a big price jump but there's a good reason for it. Richard is spending a great deal of time and money restoring the car. "The electrical system, the radiator, and the instrumentation were missing. The body was gone, except for the hood." Richard is rebuilding many of the car's parts. These pictures show a few of those rebuilt parts.

The original windscreen was gone. Richard built this one out of brass. It will be chrome-plated before the car is finished.

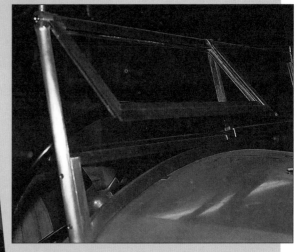

"Walter Owen Bentley spent a great deal of money doing engine development. He used a particularly light metal — magnesium-aluminum alloy — in the engine. This kept the weight of a very large engine to a minimum."

All in a day's work

"All my days are different, depending on what stage the cars are in and their condition," notes Richard. "Sometimes I get a whole car. Sometimes it's a box of parts. Anything is repairable if it is valuable enough. Money is always an issue. This business has changed a lot over the years — antique cars are worth a lot more money now.

"If I get an entire car, I take it apart, analyze the pieces, and put it back together again. If it's a box of parts, I have to start rebuilding."

From the ground up

Richard starts with what is left of the car's frame. He may have to make a plywood and wire model to send to the carpenters. The carpenters — called "coach builders" in the car industry — build a wood frame for the car. "You need artistic skills to make these models. You also have to enjoy doing it. It is a lot of work."

When a car doesn't have to be rebuilt from the ground up, it skips the carpenter's shop. Richard will usually send it to the "panel beater" — the person who makes the car's metal body. This is a very specialized profession, and there are very few panel beaters in North America.

Making it run

In his own shop, Richard concentrates on the chassis. First he rebuilds the engine, then the rest of the chassis. "I do all the wiring, put the fuel tank in, and install the brakes. I have to build an exhaust system and everything else that it needs to make it run." Richard laughs. "Then I drive this 'skeleton' up and down the road in front of my house to make sure it works before I put the body on. I get some strange looks!"

Castings

To rebuild an antique car, Richard needs to replace many of the metal parts. Some he finds in catalogues specializing in antique cars and car parts, but some just aren't made any more. When that is the case, Richard has to build the part himself, using a process called casting.

The metal casting is rough when it comes out of the mold. Richard tools (trims) it so that it matches the original metal part.

First, Richard carves pieces of wood to make a model of the part. Since most metal parts are hollow, a wooden "core" carving also has to be done. The wooden pieces are used to make a mold in sand. Liquid metal is poured into the mold.

On the left is the original part, in the middle is Richard's carved wooden model, and on the right is the new, replacement casting.

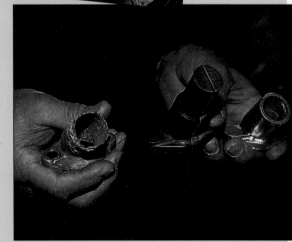

Finishing touches

Once Richard has checked to make sure all the pieces of the body and chassis fit together, he sends the exterior body parts to be painted. From the painter, the body and chassis are taken to an upholsterer to have the seats and other interior surfaces finished. "They have finally started reproducing the right type of leather for the seats. For a long time I couldn't get it.

"Sometimes I think that all I do is move cars," chuckles Richard. For example, today he has two cars at

"Bentleys have always been luxury cars. Back in 1930, a Bentley cost about $20 000 and a Ford cost $300."

the panel beater's, four at the painter's, one at the upholsterer's, and the parts of several others in his shop. "And none of them are ready to drive yet!"

Where do all those cars go?

Some of the cars Richard restores are actually sent back to Europe. "Many older cars — from the 1920s and 1930s — were destroyed in World War II. A lot of those that survived were exported to North America. They are very rare in Europe. So Europeans are now buying their antique cars here." When Richard has finished renovating a car, it is loaded into a container. The container goes by rail to an east coast port and then by ship to Europe.

Activity

Repairs required

Repairing antique cars, or any car, takes a lot of time, money, and thought. Part of the process involves problem-solving — finding the best method to use for each repair. You can go through the same process as Richard does by designing your own repair method.

You will need
- an aluminum pie plate
- scissors
- an assortment of repair materials, such as masking tape, glue, staples, rivets, crimping tools, etc.
- an assortment of finishing materials, such as spray paint, sand paper, etc.

Procedure
1. In the middle of your pie plate, cut a triangular hole large enough to put three fingers through.

Challenge

Visit a local automotive supply store. Ask the salesperson to show you the products available to repair small holes in the metal body of a car. Read each product label. Do any of them use a method similar to what you used to repair the hole in your plate? Are the materials similar? Did you find any methods you could have used to repair your plate?

2. Now, think about how you could repair the hole in your plate. You may want to test various materials and methods before you find one you think might work. Test your repair:
- the plate must be able to hold water without leaking for five minutes;
- you must not be able to see the outline of the original hole.

How to become a car restorer

"You have to love old cars to do this type of work," Richard says simply. He started working with cars very early. "I bought my first car when I was 16. It was a 1949 MGTC roadster. (A roadster is a convertible without side windows.) I could have bought a nearly-new car for the money, but I wanted that one. I took that car apart and put it back together. I really enjoyed it. I drove that car for about four years, through Chicago winters, with no heater. I got frostbite on my hands."

After finishing school, Richard worked as a commercial artist for several years. He wasn't happy doing that, so he and a friend decided to open their own garage to service sports cars. "We both had tools and the skills we needed. But we had to come up with a month's

rent for a building." After running a successful business for several years, the partners split. "He was more interested in servicing cars. I wanted to do restorations."

Richard says he learned a lot of what he knows about cars and restoring them from the people he

Richard needs very specialized skills to work on Bentleys, but many of these skills can be applied to newer cars as well.

employed in his business. "Any young person wanting to enter the business should pay attention to what experienced people say and teach," he advises. "There are classes in most high schools that can get you started, but you need to work with someone who enjoys the history of the cars to learn about restoration. Look for a shop where the owner wants an apprentice right out of high school."

There are not a lot of people doing the type of restoration that Richard does. And for a very good reason. "You don't find many old cars any more." He adds, however, that there is a definite market for the "new" old cars of the 1950s, 1960s, and 1970s.

Is this career for you?

Sometimes Richard has to say no to a customer. It's a lesson he learned the hard way. "I had a customer who wanted me to restore a car in a way that was not historically correct," he recalls. "I did the job, and now it keeps coming back to haunt me. Every time the owner takes that car to a show, he doesn't say that's how he ordered it. He just says that's how I did it. I have to explain about that car to just about everyone I meet. Now, I do restoration the way it *should* be done. If I'm pleased with a car, then everyone else will be pleased with it."

Richard also points out that anyone interested in working in this field should probably start in a garage, as a mechanic or doing body work. "Not many people do what I do. It takes a while to become your own boss."

Reading blueprints and following them precisely are a necessary part of Richard's job. "You need good math skills for this," he notes.

Career planning

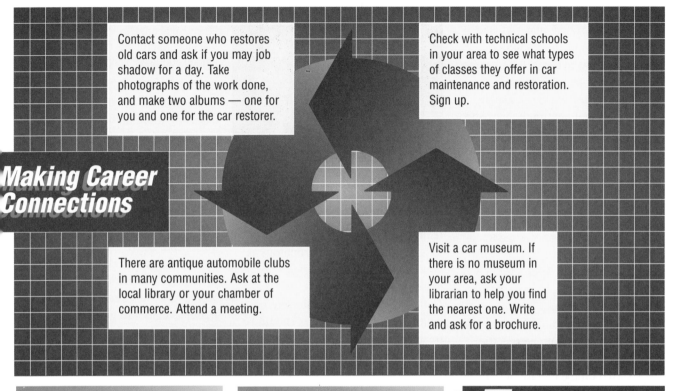

Contact someone who restores old cars and ask if you may job shadow for a day. Take photographs of the work done, and make two albums — one for you and one for the car restorer.

Check with technical schools in your area to see what types of classes they offer in car maintenance and restoration. Sign up.

Making Career Connections

There are antique automobile clubs in many communities. Ask at the local library or your chamber of commerce. Attend a meeting.

Visit a car museum. If there is no museum in your area, ask your librarian to help you find the nearest one. Write and ask for a brochure.

Getting started

Interested in becoming an antique car restorer? Here's what you can do now.

1. Take plenty of math courses. You will need math skills to read a blueprint or to cast a reproduction piece.
2. Read antique auto magazines to see the different kinds of cars being restored. What types appeal to you?
3. Learn about the skills needed to renovate an antique car. Most schools have classes in auto repair and refinishing.
4. Apply for a part-time job in a garage. Many skills are best learned from experienced people.
5. Join an antique car club. You may be able to help other people work on their cars.
6. Drawing skills are very useful. Take art classes in school and work on developing your artistic eye.

Related careers

Here are some related careers you may want to check out.

Mechanic
Repairs and maintains the engines and drive trains of cars. Must understand the different engine types in different makes of cars.

Coach builder
Uses carpentry skills in car restoration. Builds interior framing for bodies, doors, and seats. May make dashboards and trim from fine woods.

Upholsterer
Builds or reupholsters household furniture. May specialize in upholstering seats and inside panels in cars, vans, and motor homes.

Metal fabricator
Makes metal objects by casting, forging, welding, or soldering. May work for car restorers, farm service companies, or machine shops. May make craft items to sell at craft shows.

Future watch

The definition of "old" is changing. Cars from the 1950s, 1960s, and 1970s are now being restored as antique automobiles. The interest in these cars is growing. Auto shows and museums have grown in number and size over the last few decades. More jobs are becoming available, not only in car restoration but in supplying the parts needed to do a restoration. "There is also a lot of work in aircraft and boat restoration," says Richard.

Dawn Hill — Cultural Anthropologist

Anthropologists study the physical, social, material, and cultural development of human beings. With so many different areas to study, most anthropologists specialize in just one field. Dawn Hill is a cultural anthropologist. She studies the cultures of humans: the way each group of people lives that makes it different from any other group.

The way anthropologists study the world appeals to Dawn. "This is the only discipline that allows me to travel all over the world. I can visit with the people I'm interested in and learn from them. That's what makes what I do so exciting."

Cultural anthropologists often learn and write about one specific group of people. Right now, Dawn has focused on the culture of one group of Native North Americans — the Lubicon Cree.

"In the past, anthropology has often misrepresented aboriginal cultures. There have been some

really wrong ideas expressed. I want to help change how anthropology is done in relation to aboriginal traditions. I want to make sure the Native voice and the Elders are not belittled. Their knowledge should be treated with respect."

Getting to know people

"There are two aspects to what I do: research and sharing what I've learned with others." To do her research, Dawn asked for permission to live in the Lubicon Cree community and record their cultural traditions. "They tell their story. All I do is write it down. I'm only a 'facilitator,' getting this information

In addition to teaching and research, Dawn helps organize conferences and meetings to promote communication among aboriginal people.

to the public." Dawn shares what she learns by teaching her students and by writing articles and books.

Study, study, and study some more

To do what Dawn does takes many years of study and a great deal of work. Like Dawn, most cultural anthropologists work for a college or university. This requires a Bachelor's degree, and then several years in graduate school to get both a Master's and Doctorate (Ph.D.) degree.

"If you want to pursue a career in this area, it is important that you enjoy meeting and getting to know people," advises Dawn. "You have to like people to be a cultural anthropologist. Your research demands that you talk to strangers."

Cultural differences

There are many cultural differences between human cultures, some very subtle. The easiest ones to discover are visual. For example, in many Asian countries, people wear white when someone dies. In European cultures, black is traditional for mourning.

Dawn has spent time living in the Lubicon Cree community and has helped organize conferences and meetings among aboriginal people.

Getting started

1. Start learning about other cultures now. Watch television documentaries and read about other cultures.
2. Talk to people in your school who are from other cultures. Learn how their traditions differ from your own.
3. Study a foreign language in school.
4. Does your school have classes for students who are learning to speak English? Offer to help tutor. You'll learn about other cultures as you do.

Jim Retallack — History Professor

Everyone knows that history tells you exactly what happened in the past, right? Not always, says Jim Retallack. Jim teaches history at a large university. He says that there may be many interpretations about what happened. Getting students to realize this is one of the hardest things to teach.

"I try to tell them that not all historians agree about what happened. Many students don't want to hear that. They want the right answer. But most of the time, there is no right answer.

"History can be different things according to different people," says

Jim spends part of his time working alone in his office, and the other part teaching students.

Jim. "That is what makes being a historian so interesting. You make up your own mind about what happened, based on the material you find."

Doing history

Jim's work falls into two areas: research and teaching. Research, from a historian's viewpoint, means investigating what happened, and then telling it or writing about it. Historians investigate by looking at many written records (diaries, letters, newspapers) and other clues (paintings, buildings) that have survived. Then they try to piece together all the clues into a picture of what really happened at a certain time in the past.

The big problem is that not everything from the past still exists. Historians have to puzzle out what happened without knowing all the details.

Reading old documents is also not easy. Historians often have to understand more than one language. Also, many old documents are handwritten. That means deciphering the handwriting (and sometimes an entirely

different alphabet), in order to read what the document says.

The second and equally important job of many historians — particularly those who work in schools — is to teach what they know to students. "Teaching is not just getting across a body of knowledge. It is also getting students interested in how to study history. Then, they can find out for themselves what happened in the past." To do Jim's job, you need to have a Ph.D. in history. Historians with Bachelor's and Master's degrees often work for archives and libraries.

What materials do historians use?

In their research, historians use both "primary sources" and "secondary sources." A primary source is something left behind by the people who were there. It can be a diary, a letter, a newspaper, or a government memo.

Secondary sources are books or articles written about a particular period in history. These sources are usually the author's interpretation of what happened at the time.

The date of this German newspaper (24 September 1914) was about seven weeks after the start of the First World War. Is it a primary source or a secondary source?

Getting started

1. Is there a country or time period that interests you? Start reading about it now!
2. Study at least one other language.
3. Go to a meeting of a local historical society. You'll meet others who have similar interests.
4. Apply for a summer job at a local historical site as a tour guide.

Susan Steer — Title Searcher

A title searcher finds out about the history of a piece of land — who owns it, who owned it in the past, how often it was sold, and how much it was sold for. Susan Steer is a self-employed title searcher. She works in a registry office, a government office where land ownership is registered. Every time a piece of property is sold, the change in ownership, called change in "title," is officially recorded.

Searching the history

"When someone wants to buy a piece of property, their lawyer phones and asks me to check out who actually owns it," explains Susan. "This is called 'searching the title' to the property. I do this for a lot of house sales, as usually a house and land are sold together."

"The first thing I do when I search a title is to find the piece of land by its legal description. This information is kept in a reference book at the registry office. Then, I check that the person who is selling the land is the same person listed as the owner." If it is — and it usually is — then Susan has to certify that the seller has "clear title." That means that the seller really owns the property, there are no violations of building codes, and no money is owed against the property to anyone else. If this is not the case, Susan must report her findings to the lawyer.

If everything is in order and the sale takes place, Susan then does all the necessary paperwork to register the new owner.

"I've found some interesting things in the older records. I came across one piece of property that had belonged to a man who had drowned in 1840. When his heirs sold the property in 1911, they had to explain what happened to him. They recorded that he had dizzy spells and fell out of a boat."

Getting into the land business

Susan says she became interested in this career when she was in high school. "I thought about law but I didn't want to spend years in school to be a lawyer. I also knew I didn't want to be a legal secretary. I talked to my school guidance counselor and he suggested that I look at title searching. Now, high schools have law classes and many colleges have legal assistant programs.

"Most title searchers start by working for a law firm. A lot of law firms hire young people and train them to their way of doing things. After a few years, many searchers go out on their own, as I did. But you need a network of contacts to get a good jump in your own business."

Getting started

1. Talk to your school guidance counselor. Ask about legal careers and what courses are offered at the high school level and after.
2. Talk to a title searcher in your area. Look in the Yellow Pages under "Searchers of Records" or "Title Searchers."
3. Study legal terms, especially those that apply to land.
4. Go to your local registry office and find the legal description of the piece of land your school sits on. Look up who owned the land in the past.

Why do a title search?

Is all this paperwork and expense really necessary? "Yes," says Susan. "Anybody can buy and sell a piece of property, but if they don't register the sale, the ownership hasn't changed." That means that until the government has a record that you bought a piece of land, you don't legally own it.

Barklay Holmes — Antique Dealer

"Being an antique dealer is more than buying and selling tables, chairs, and pretty tea sets," says Barclay Holmes, an antique dealer who owns his own shop. "I also buy and sell period artifacts. These can be many different things: architectural details (such as fireplace mantels or doors and wood work from old buildings); fine artworks (such as paintings or sculpture); and the usual furniture and china.

"When you own your own shop," explains Barclay, "You do many things. I travel to find items and visit my clients to talk about their possessions. About the only thing that is consistent in my days are the store's hours. Everything else varies, depending on the needs of my customers."

"My day usually starts in the late morning. I go on a tour of about four shops that I call my 'traplines,' to see if they have anything that would be of interest to my clients.

"Then I open the shop in the afternoon. There can be one or two customers or twenty. When the shop is open, I'm busy answering questions and explaining what things are. In the evenings, I do deliveries. Or I go out and examine pieces that someone is selling, or needs appraised for insurance."

Spotting the imposters

Because of his experience, Barclay is able to tell if a piece is a fake or a copy. "For example, how a piece is assembled is a good clue. Hand tools leave different marks than machine tools do. Things that have dowels are easy to assess." (Dowels are

Just by looking at an antique, Barklay can usually tell his clients how rare it is and what it is worth.

small pieces of wood used to join larger pieces of wood together, like table legs to frames.) "Modern furniture uses round dowels. Old furniture used square dowels in round holes. The dowels were driven in by force and the pressure locked them in place. There was no need to use glue. If a piece has round dowels in round holes, it probably isn't that old."

Getting into the business

Barclay advises any young person who wants to work in this business to start early. "You must have a real love of antiques and artifacts. You also have to be prepared to start small, and slowly build your collection. Most antique dealers begin buying and selling while they hold other jobs.

"Antique dealing is almost like the medical profession. You have to develop a sixth sense."

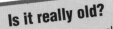

Is it really old?

There are many clues to the age and origin of an antique. This plate has several clues in its markings. First, study the picture on the front of the plate. What is shown there? Can you recognize the city in the background? Do the marks on the back of the plate tell you anything? The answers are on page 48.

Getting started

1. Look around your home for old dishes, tools, or furniture. Examine the markings. Look them up at the library.
2. Go to antique shows. Ask an antique dealer to tell you about his or her specialty.
3. History, math, and courses on running your own business will help provide the skills you need.

Classified Advertising

Help Wanted

Who got the job?

Finding a job

The first step to success in any career is getting a job. But how do you go about finding one?

- In almost every field, many jobs are advertised by word-of-mouth. Talk with family, friends, neighbors, and teachers and let them know what jobs interest you.

- Respond to "Help Wanted" ads in newspapers.

- Post an advertisement of your skills on a community bulletin board.

- Contact potential employers by phone or in person. Volunteer your services if no paying jobs are immediately available.

- Send out inquiry letters to companies and agencies, and follow up with phone calls.

A job application usually consists of a letter and a resumé (a summary of your experience and qualifications for the job). Applicants whose resumés show they are qualified may be invited to a job interview.

Activity

Getting a summer job

A local museum coordinator was looking for summer help. She placed the advertisement shown on the opposite page in a local newspaper.

A job in the museum is attractive, not only to those interested in the past but also to anyone hoping to work in museums in the future. There were many qualified applicants for the job but Ellen Watkins only interviewed the best candidates. Two of these were Lee Ogino and Terry Garcia. Their letters and resumés, and the notes, made by Ellen Watkins as the interviews were in progress, are shown on pages 46 and 47.

Procedure

Make a list of the qualifications that you think are important for a good tour guide. Now consider each applicant's resumé, cover letter, and performance during the job interview. Determine how well each one matched the requirements that you wrote on your list. Which candidate has better qualifications and experience?

Whom do you think Ellen Watkins should hire for the job: Lee or Terry? Was there any outstanding reason

Challenge

How would you perform in a job interview? Role-play an interview, with a friend or member of your family playing the part of Ellen Watkins. Then reverse roles. This practice can help you be more confident when you have your first real interview. It is important to feel relaxed, and rehearsing will help you to feel comfortable.

why you would choose not to hire one candidate? In your judgment, what were the most important qualities of the candidate that you chose?

Lee Ogino's application and interview

556 West 57th Street
Harriton, Province/State
Postal/Zip Code

May 22, 19—

Ms. Ellen Watkins
Heritage Museum
433 Main Street
Harriton, Province/State
Postal/Zip Code

Dear Ms. Watkins,

I would like to apply for the summer tour guide position advertised in the Harriton Journal. I have always had an interest in the past. When I was six, my grandmother gave me five old quilts that had been in the family for many years. Since then I have added several quilts to my collection and learned a great deal about quilt making and antique patterns and fabrics.

I will enter my final year at Harriton High School in the fall and plan to enrol in an undergraduate program in anthropology after graduation. Someday I would like to work in a museum, possibly as a textile conservator.

Thank you for considering my application. If you would like further information, please call me at 555-8890.

Sincerely,

Lee Ogino

Lee Ogino

Interview: Lee Ogino

- *arrived on time, dressed neatly in jacket and slacks.*

- *very business-like and courteous, but a bit stiff. Shyness may be a problem.*

- *understood the importance of tour guide's job in public relations.*

- *expressed an interest in textiles on display. Has good general knowledge of fabric and the quilting traditions shown in the collection.*

Resumé
Lee Ogino
556 West 57th Street
Harriton, Province/State
Postal/Zip Code
Phone: 555-8890

Education:
Entering my final year at Harriton High School i the fall. My best subjects are history and math

Work Experience:
Babysitting: Full-time for the two children of M Ann Simons. Ages: four and two. Summer 19—, evenings and weekends
Lawn care: Have assisted several neighbors with mowing, weeding, and other lawn care work for the past three years.

Volunteering:
Worked full-time last summer on the renovation the Old Harriton Community House, a designated historical site.

Interests:
Collecting antique quilts.
Member of the Harriton High School Drum and Bugl Corp.
Reading, quilting, music.

References:
Available upon request.

Terry Garcia's application and interview

688 Applebee Lane
Harriton, Province/State
Postal/Zip Code

May 22, 19—

Ms. Ellen Watkins
Heritage Museum
433 Main Street
Harriton, Province/State
Postal/Zip Code

Dear Ms. Watkins,

Please allow me to introduce myself. My name is Terry Garcia and I would like to apply for the tour guide position with Heritage Museum.

As you can see from my resumé, I have considerable experience in working with antiques. I also have experience in public speaking and sales. I believe these would be assets in a museum tour guide.

I am enclosing my resumé with this letter. Thank you for your time. If you have any other questions, I can be reached at 555-2233, after school hours and on weekends.

Sincerely,

Terry Garcia

Terry Garcia

Interview: Terry Garcia

- *arrived early, dressed neatly in jacket and slacks.*
- *very relaxed and personable. Makes a very good first impression.*
- *obviously at ease with people. Debating and sales skills evident.*
- *knows something about antiques but thinks he knows more than he does.*

Resumé
Terry Garcia
688 Applebee Lane
Harriton, Province/State
Postal/Zip Code
Telephone: 555-2233

Employment: Part-time assistant at Garcia's Antiques (parents' store). Duties included helping customers, using the cash register, unpacking and stocking merchandise, and cleaning.

Education: I will be entering my final year at Harriton High School in the fall. I plan to attend college following graduation.

Activities: Member of the Harriton High Tennis Team. Member of the Harriton High Debate Society. First place in extemporaneous speaking, High School Debate Tournament, 19—.

Interests: Mountain biking, baseball, reading science fiction books.

References: On request.

Index

Answers

The plate is from a set made in the 1830s by a British company called Davenport. If you look at the plate in the right light, you can just see Davenport's name stamped into the clay, just above the word "Montreal" on the back. (You may not be able to see the name in this photograph.) "Montreal" is both the name of the dinnerware pattern and the name of the city in the background of the picture on the front. In the 1830s, the St. Lawrence River and Montreal looked as they do on the front of the plate. The steamship, the "British American," was a real ship on the St. Lawrence at this time.

Credits

(l = left; r = right; t = top; b = bottom; c = center; bl = bottom left; br = bottom right)

All art by Warren Clark. All photographs by Victoria Vincent, except 5(r), 6, 7(t), 8(t) The Royal Ontario Museum; 12(tl, tr, bl), 14(b) Jon Jouppien; 14(t); 17, 18(t, c), 19, 20b Jennifer Dunn; 20(t); 29, 30(b), 31 Charlotte Dean; 30(t), 32(t) Sharon McCormick; 37 from The Automobile: The First Century by David Burgess Wise, et al.; 41(t) Jim Retallack.